I Did
NOT
Choose This
Adventure

by Catherine L. Haws

I Did NOT Choose This Adventure

Cover and illustrations by Emily "Harpley" Steadman

Author Photo by Haws Photography

ISBN 978-1-6671-8619-1

To Katie
and to everyone else
who has believed in me.

The Known Lands
LONE SPIRE
The Westley Mountains
Dragon Country

Contents

Chapter 1

Atypical Tuesday

I became a Kingdom Sentry because my sisters told me I should get out more.

Although they said standing outside wasn't quite what they meant, I liked the job: Tuesdays and Thursdays from one to three in the afternoon.

At that time of day, the kingdom generally took a nap. This made my job easier since there wouldn't be any shady characters to make trouble if they were all taking naps.

The position only existed because Princess Chelseanna had announced she would return from her quest by way of the West Gate, and the king wanted the gate manned at all hours. All the other sentries said that by now the princess was either hopelessly lost or eaten by a dragon.

Either way, I still had my quiet afternoons to myself.

One typical Tuesday, I leaned against the archway of the gate snacking on a slice of cheese when a lone, shady figure in the distance caught my attention.

I had never encountered any shady figures before, so I stiffened.

All right, Reggie, I said to myself. *Remember what they said in the Kingdom Sentry Training Seminar: "Be the Sentry of the Century."*

The figure dragged a cart like a snail lugging a shell.

"Who goes there?" I called out.

The figure stopped for a moment then shouted back, "I do."

We stood in silence.

Then, with some new burst of vigor, the figure picked up the cart again and headed straight toward me.

I felt for my sword hilt with one hand and shielded my eyes with the other. If he indeed meant trouble, I'd have to fend him off single-handedly: one, because everyone else was home napping, and two, because I'd need my other hand to keep shielding my eyes from the sun.

A meandering path of shiny, black ooze, dripped out of the cart trailing behind like a slithering snail trail. The figure wore a shadowy hood and bedraggled boots.

Once the hooded figure came closer, I inquired, "Why are you pulling that cart?"

"My horse was eaten."

The figure stopped a few paces in front of me and set down the cart shafts. More black ooze leaked from under the tarp that covered the cart and rippled into a puddle.

The edge of the figure's hood glistened with subtle, silver embroidery. Stretching with a yawn, the figure leaned back, and the hood fell, revealing long, dark hair in need of a good brushing, and a brown, scab-freckled face I recognized.

"Princess Chelseanna!" I knelt at once. "You've returned from your quest!"

"I sure have," she said, looking behind her at the cart. From my vantage point, I could see something white and dirty under the tarp. "Meet Maximus Khanivorous Smelter the Third!"

She cast off the canvas tarp, revealing an enormous, severed eyeball of a dragon. It glared directly down at me with fiery vengeance.

I fainted.

As I blinked awake, the princess leaned over me, her ratty hair brushing my neck, and she repeatedly flicked my forehead.

"Wake up!"

I groaned.

"So much for a joyous homecoming." She pulled me to my feet. "Run and wake Daddy from his nap. Let him know," she took in a breath, gazing at the surrounding kingdom, "I'm back."

* * *

The king threw a typical slain-dragon party. The whole kingdom celebrated by feasting, dancing, and competing in cheese carving contests. The dragon's eye was displayed behind glass on a crystal pedestal.

I guarded the doorway between the billiard room and the refreshments during the festivities.

After the royal family bade the guests good night, the king and princess began a game of pool. The bustle of departing guests quieted as they began filtering out.

All night I had been eyeing the refreshments. The towers of stacked cheese tantalized me but were just out of reach.

While I considered the logistics of skewering a medium-sized round of cheddar on my sword, the princess and the king chatted over their game of pool.

"I figure that raiding the Fountain of Eternal Youth won't be so difficult after slaying a dragon," the king said.

"That's easy for you to say," the princess replied and sent the balls cracking against one another. "I'm not saying I can't do it—you know I'm always game for a quest—I just don't know if the Fountain is worth it."

"Not worth it?" the king said in disbelief. "Why not, Chelly?"

"I think you would hate living forever, Daddy."

"Me?" The king laughed. "*I* don't want to *drink* it! What a waste! No, we shall use it on the castle. Can you imagine the opportunities if it never crumbles and ages? Never having to pay for the upkeep! Think of the tourism in two hundred years!"

"By Jove!" the princess exclaimed. "Daddy, that's the most forethoughtful idea I've ever heard!"

While they were carrying on this discussion, I had unsheathed my sword and punctured a round of cheese with the tip of my blade. With care, I gripped the hilt with both hands and leaned in for leverage.

To my dismay, the blade swung like the arm of a catapult, sending the cheese careening through the air!

In utter anguish, I watched the entire trajectory of the cheese from the tip of my blade to the face of the unsuspecting king.

Chapter 2

How I Got into This Quest

The king and the projectile cheese fell to the floor with a thump. The princess and I stared down at him then looked up at each other.

I could almost hear the booming toll of my impending fate: *You're fired!*

I considered running to the nearest broom closet to hide.

"You!" the princess exclaimed.

I froze, preparing for the words.

Narrowing her eyes, the princess said, "You've heard our entire conversation, haven't you?" I grimaced and slowly shrugged. I took a breath to plead for mercy, but she interrupted and said, "Word of this quest mustn't get around." She tightened her grip on her cue stick and scrutinized me up and down. "Actually, you might do."

Might do what? I wondered.

On the floor, the king grabbed the cheese and took a generous bite. "Quite a shot, young man!" he said, rubbing his nose. The princess turned and helped him to his feet.

"It was an accident!" I said.

"Even better!" the king laughed.

"That settles it," the princess said. "You're hired!"

"What?" I said.

"We depart on Thursday."

"Thursday?" the king said. "So soon?"

"Well," the princess nudged the king with her elbow, "the castle ain't gettin' any younger!" She set down her cue stick and rubbed her hands together. "No time like the present to start planning! See you then—"

"But I work on Thursdays," I said, numb from the shock.

"Daddy can write you up an excuse form!" She passed by me then stopped and spun around. "Who are you anyway?"

I fixed my posture and bowed. "Reginald Fitzhamlet the Seventh, Your Majesty."

She raised an eyebrow. "That's a long name!"

"Most people call me Reggie," I said, bowing again.

"All right, Reggie, Thursday morning, bright-eyed and bushy-tailed!"

11

* * *

On Wednesday when my family heard about the quest, the house erupted like a kicked hornets nest. My sisters swarmed around me and bombarded me with questions from all sides.

"What?"

"When?"

"Why?"

"How?"

Half of them told me *not* to go: "Our family has a bad history with quests, you know!"

Half of them told me I *should* go: "You could change the family's bad history with quests!"

Once the squabble calmed down, Mother and Father said that since the princess gave the order, it should be followed.

At that, everyone pitched in. Mother darned the holes in my socks, Father polished my shoes, Norma borrowed books from the library for me, the twins (Gladys and Phyllis) made me hardtack crackers, and Tilly spread the news to my oldest two sisters and their husbands.

Caught up in the frenzy, I rushed to the Sentry Center. However, getting any of the sentries to cover my shift at the West Gate was a harrowing undertaking. No one volunteered to help me. They all balked and complained until I was convinced they wouldn't let me go at all, but then they remembered the official excuse signed by the king.

I asked if they had any advice about leaving the kingdom, but since none of them had ever left the kingdom themselves, and we never had any questing instructions in the training seminar, they just pointed to the banner with the adage I knew by heart:

"The Darefull be Careful!"

That night I burned through three candles. I studied Norma's books from the library about dragon-battling techniques, poisonous berries, and the proper ways to fold clothes for a long journey.

All that reading swam around in my head and only made me feel more nervous and ill-prepared than before. I had already folded and refolded my clothes five times, and I couldn't decide how many provisions to pack.

After the party, the king had encouraged me to take as many cheeses as I wanted; I only took seven, so as not to be rude. I do *love* cheese.

I decided to pack all of them. The princess never did mention how long this quest was supposed to take. Her last one took six months. Who knew how much cheese I might need?

When I finally blew out the candle and lay down, my thoughts from the past two days settled into view.

In my whole life I never wanted to embark on a quest!

Was I supposed to be excited?

I wasn't.

I turned over.

The Fitzhamlets have a bad history with quests. Old Reginald the First went on a quest once, and he never came back.

What if I never came back?

I turned again.

They said I should get out more.

Well, they got their wish.

In the lonely darkness, I sank into sleep.

* * *

Thursday morning, I arrived at the back door of the castle bleary eyed and shabby tailed. While standing there all alone, anxious thoughts crept into my mind.

Why did she pick ME to go on this quest? The only experience I had with facing any unsavory characters outside of the Training Seminar was Tuesday afternoon and that turned out to be the princess herself! What if I told her she'd be better off finding someone else?

The back door of the castle burst open.

"I'll be back if I survive," the princess hollered behind her. "Keep an eye out for me at the West Gate!" With that, she slammed the door and shoved an empty glass jug into my arms. "Hold this." She adjusted her drawstring knapsack and pulled her hair out from under the straps.

"Your Majesty," I said, mentally preparing my resignation speech.

"You don't have to call me 'Your Majesty;' it takes too long." She began walking, and I trailed behind her, still carrying the jug.

"All right then, uh, Princess Chelseanna—"

"Good heavens, that's even longer! Just call me Chel."

"Very well, uh, Chel, if I may be so bold—"

"Please, do. We are beginning a quest after all!" She chuckled and sped along even faster. "Boldness is indeed one of my favorite qualities in a person. Sniveling cowards who refuse to even try are missing out on the vast greatness the world has to offer!" She stretched out her arms with vivacious enthusiasm. "Now," she said, turning to look back at me, "what was it you wanted to ask?"

"Umm…" I gulped, "I wanted to ask…where are we going?"

"The Sea."

"Is that where the Fountain of Eternal—"

"SHHHH!" Princess Chel spun around and pressed a finger to my lips. I almost dropped the jug. "The secrecy of our quest must be upheld! Do not mention the You Know What by its name. EVER!" She squinted and looked cautiously around. "We never know who may be listening. No one must know what we're after!"

Chapter 3

Not-So-Smooth Sailing

I followed in silence as we strode through the mostly empty streets. My bag began to weigh heavily on my shoulders, as did the reality that I was leaving home.

Princess Chel led the way to the North End. Salty air stung my nostrils.

She looked skyward and hummed wistfully. "I do love a good quest!" She glanced back at me. I attempted a half-hearted smile, but the jug slipped a bit in my sweaty hands. "CAREFUL!" She supported the opposite side of the jug. "This is the Bolli-hydrium Urn of Fathomless Depths! A whole ocean can be captured inside this very urn!"

The urn seemed to burn my hands with urgency.

"Then why am *I* holding it?!"

"I didn't want it getting smashed by my helmet, tent poles, and weapons." She gestured a thumb to her knapsack.

I blinked. "You've got all that in there?"

"Tell you what." She slung her remarkably small knapsack over one shoulder. "Dump all your stuff in here and put the urn in your bag."

I obeyed as ordered, a trifle embarrassed as she raised an eyebrow at my collection of cheeses, and all the contents dropped easily down in the open mouth of her drawstring knapsack.

"Might as well stick in your sword, so it won't weigh you down," she added.

I obliged and asked, "Is your knapsack fathomless too?"

"Almost." She cinched it up and shoved the urn into my bag. It took up all the space inside. "Royalty has its perks."

As we continued through the streets, the fish markets presented full baskets of fresh catches, steam fogged the bakery windows, and seagulls circled above us with mocking calls.

"Are we going on a voyage?" A knot was developing in my stomach. "I've never been sailing."

"We'll be sailing all right," the princess said, leading the way down a dock, "but it's a dinghy." We stopped in front of what looked like a one-person, toy sailboat.

"Where shall I sit?" I asked.

"Up front. Just watch your head when the sail swings. Hope you know how to swim."

"I don't."

"Really? I thought they trained sentries how to swim. 'Darefull be Careful' and all that!"

"Well, they said better to be careful and not dare to swim at all."

She tsked, shook her head, and climbed down into the boat.

* * *

After about two hours of clinging to the mast for dear life, dodging and failing to dodge the swift sail, and almost inadvertently capsizing

22

the vessel four times, I ventured to ask, "Why exactly are we going to sea?" I feared that if we kept heading into the open ocean, we'd have to spend the night. I tried to imagine what a tent pitched on the dinghy might look like.

"We are going to pay a visit to the mermaids," she said.

Images of fanged teeth, icy eyes, siren calls, and sunken ships flashed into my imagination, and I gasped with horror.

"B-b-but they're pirates!"

"Exactly!" She smiled. "And what do pirates have?"

"Evil intentions!" I hissed.

"Well, I guess so, but they also have treasure."

"Do they have the—*You Know What?*"

She laughed at me. "Of course not! The *You Know What* is in the Westley Mountains."

23

"Then why are we sailing at all?"

"To find seven golden griffin claw tips."

She frowned at my confusion and dug in her knapsack. She withdrew an old map unrolling it between us.

There in faded ink were, on one side, the Kingdom, the Sea, and the Formidable Forrest. On the other side were the Westley Mountains. At the bottom, two arrows pointed downward beside the words, "Dragon Country."

A gaping burned hole took up the entire center of the map leaving only a thin frame like a crust of bread. The pit in the map matched the pit in my stomach.

"The best way to get from here to there," she pointed from the kingdom over the hole to the red X marked in the mountains, "is unknown, because we don't know what lies between here and there. So, our best bet is to hire some griffins to fly us there."

"Griffins?!" I pictured a stern-looking, sneering eagle with the hind end of a lion crouching ready to pounce. "Aren't griffins rather, um…"

"Formidable? Yes, but if you get on their good side, they can be fierce and loyal. Legend has it that offering seven golden griffin claw tips will land you on their good side."

"What exactly do griffins do with golden claw tips?"

"I have no idea. Put them on like thimbles, I guess." She pulled up on the rope and the boat slowed to drifting. "Hear that?"

A smooth and eerie music echoed beneath the glassy, bluish water. In the distance, there laid a green shore lined with trees, and two thin bands of rocks forming a wide bay.

"Welcome to the lagoon of the Merpirates."

Chapter 4

What Happened to the Hose

"I'm going to put on my diving suit," Princess Chel said, so matter-of-factly that, at first, I didn't panic. As soon as she began digging in her knapsack, however, I turned away, twiddling my thumbs around the mast, and fixed my gaze on the distant trees on the shoreline. Behind me, clangs and thumps vibrated the boat.

"Reggie, I need your help with the straps and laces."

A terrified drop of sweat clung to my brow.

Whenever my elder sisters readied themselves for dances, I was expelled to the gloomy basement to give them privacy. All alone, I dressed and attempted to knot my own tie, but since there was no mirror in the basement, all I had to examine my reflection were glass jars of canned tomatoes.

Before departure, my sisters enlisted my help to tie their dancing shoes—with strict orders to only look down as they lifted their skirts.

My own tie, however, never turned out right and in the end, was always redone by one of my sisters at the last minute. I blame the tomato jars.

I've never liked tomatoes or gloomy places anyway.

"Hurry up, and turn around, Reggie, we don't have all day!"

With a gulp, I turned to face the princess. I almost slid off the boat in surprise. She wore a canvas-like, full body, toe-to-neck suit complete with mittens and a metal helmet connected by a riveted shoulder plate.

In one hand she held a trident. A little window in the helmet hung open showing her eyes and nose.

"I need you to tie the leg and wrist laces and strap tight the air hose. The suit's a little big for me, so the limbs puff out underwater," she explained.

I did as she said, sweating now from the ever-rising sun, and tied the last wrist bow with a flourish. She looked at both her wrists. "Where did you learn to tie such nice bows?"

I shrugged. "I've got six older sisters."

"Good heavens!" She looked at me with a hint of pity then back down at the knots. "I've got three older brothers, and our nursemaid lost some fingers from her run-in with a dragon. I never did learn how to tie bows."

I opened my mouth to offer her a lesson, but she held up the end of a long, green tube that connected to her helmet.

"This is my air supply hose. Without it, I will drown. Whatever you do, do NOT let this air hose drop into the water!" I took it and nodded vigorously. "If my calculations and research are right," she continued, "the mermaids should be having lunch, and only a few will be guarding the treasury."

"How will you—" I began.

"Don't worry about me." She closed the little window on her helmet and secured the lever. Then, her voice traveled up through the air hose held aloft in my hand, "Don't. Drop. The hose."

With that, she sat on the edge of the boat and slid down into the water, gripping her trident, leaving me alone.

All was quiet.

Miniature waves tapped the sides of the boat making a glugging noise, and the salty air tickled the back of my throat.

I recalled the princess had mentioned lunch, and I began thinking of which cheese I might choose first.

A splash in the distance brought me back to the present moment.

The slippery music from before echoed closer, and I turned to see rippling lines of water ebbing toward me. My sentry instincts itched for the comfort of my sword.

I reached for the princess's knapsack, still carefully holding the hose in my other hand. The ripples came nearer, and I braced myself for the worst.

Vibrant colors swirled around the boat: oranges, purples, greens, and magentas. Deep, sapphire-blue faces, beaming with laughing smiles, flashed pearly white teeth. Suits of scales lengthened into tails, billowing like mesmerizing cloth in the glittering water.

Three splashes sprayed onto the boat as three heads emerged.

"Well, good afternoon!" the first said, short purple hair clinging to her dark blue face.

"It's so nice to have a visitor!" the second said, glass beads clinking in her braids like off-key wind chimes.

"What brings you to our fine waters?" the third said, batting her long green eyelashes and spreading her thin green lips in a smile.

The seminar never did teach us how to negotiate with pirates. I was on my own.

"I'd rather not say," I said, trying to pry open the princess's knapsack one handed without their notice.

"Oh, but you can tell us!"

"We won't do you any harm!"

"We just *love* meeting new people."

The three mermaids laid their elbows on the edge of the boat and rested their chins in their webbed hands.

To avoid revealing our plans, I changed the subject. "Aren't you supposed to be eating lunch?"

"What a splendid idea!" said the one with beads. "We'll join you!"

"What a gentleman!"

"What do you have?"

"Me?" I said, sinking my hand into the knapsack. I brushed aside clothes and cheeses searching for my sword. "No, I meant *your* lunch."

"You sly thing!" The green one batted her eyelashes. "Don't you know it's not very polite to invite yourself to lunch?"

"Every gentleman knows that," said the purple-haired one, turning up her nose, "especially one with shiny buttons like yours."

They all leaned in for a closer look at my uniform. The boat tilted. I dug farther into the knapsack.

"What's in that sack that's so important?"

"Oh nothing," I said.

All three of them blinked at me with flat, unamused expressions. My hand found something long and pointy.

"Well, I wanted it to be a surprise," I said, trying to be sly. "A little present for you."

I pulled my hand from the bag and swung around my weapon. A tent pole bumped across the heads of the mermaids. Their sweet smiles vanished.

So much for being sly.

The boat capsized, and I fell—air hose and all—into the water.

Chapter 5

In Which I Encounter
an Octopus

A sudden current blasted me downward, and my first thought was that the mermaids were dragging me under, but I saw they too were swept away, flailing and tumbling in the ferocious current. The top surface of the water sank with us, spinning and spinning down, down, down like a drain.

Abruptly, I crashed to the bottom with a splat. Crags of rock jutted mountain-like into the sky. Fish, in a pile at my feet, wriggled and toppled onto me.

I sat up, flinging them off, shuddering in fright. A sloshing sound behind me caused me to look over my shoulder, and I saw the neck of the urn peeking out of my bag. The entire ocean drained into the urn leaving only puddles and flopping sea dwellers.

The mermaids glared at me.

"What have you done?" they wailed, all the sweetness gone from their voices. They attempted to crawl toward me dragging their tails like wet skirts.

I grabbed Princess Chel's knapsack, scrambled to my feet, and followed the hose.

"Princess!" I called, running through avenues of rock, wrapping up the hose into her magical knapsack as I went.

Sunken ships and vacant buildings dotted the landscape of the lagoon, and if I wasn't in such a hurry, I would have paused to admire the view.

I recalled the last words she had said to me, *Don't drop the hose.*

And what had I done? Of all the moments when I couldn't be too careful, I had not been careful enough. What would she think of me now?

More mermaids wailed and shouted at me as I rounded a corner. A tangle of bright orange tentacles reached for my feet, and I leapt aside in alarm!

An agitated octopus peered up at me with severe reproach and condescension. With a twinge of compassion in my heart, I tipped out a drop from the urn, sending an ankle-deep flood. The octopus zipped past me, and I splashed forward, following the hose through a tunnel, down a hole, and out into the open again.

Towering before me stood a magnificent, stone cathedral. Drapes of sea greenery, reminiscent of climbing ivy, dripped glittering trails of water spiraling down the pillars which looked like long, elegant shells upholding the entrance arches. Shimmering mother-of-pearl bejeweled a staircase like elegant barnacles.

Why mermaids needed a staircase to the cathedral was beyond me.

Princess Chel stood under an archway with her helmet window open and her hands full of glittering gold.

"Reggie!" she shouted. "A flood of water came through the hose, drenched my face, then sucked back in, taking my air with it! You used the urn, didn't you?"

My heart sank. "Your Majesty, I'm—"

"A genius!"

"What?"

"I don't know why I didn't think to use the urn in the first place! Well done!"

I considered pointing out that I used the urn by accident but decided a more pressing matter was at hand.

"We had better hurry," I said, hopping up the steps. "We don't want to leave all the fish without water for too long."

"You're quite right." She dumped handfuls of gold into her knapsack. "This mission went more smoothly than I expected. The two treasury guards were actually glad to see me! Evidently, they haven't had any visitors for a while. They even threw in some coins for us!" She shouldered her knapsack. "Off we go!"

"What about the boat?" I said.

"We don't need it anymore."

"What about your trident?"

She planted her hands on her hips. "Those wily pirates! One of them offered to hold it while I gathered the gold. How could I have been so stupid?"

From my experience with older sisters, I knew that was the type of question where one does *not* offer an answer.

She stomped to the edge of the steps. "Well, it's too late now!" She stiffened. "What is that?"

I followed her gaze.

In the distance, an enraged mob of mermaids charged toward us—upright! Their flashing scales and flowing tails looked like ball gowns.

I was in no mood to dance.

"How do we get out of here?"

"Quick," Princess Chel said, "dump the water!"

I tipped the urn, and the ocean began to refill. In a rush of current, we floated up above the cathedral.

With the rising water rose my sense of panic.

"I can't swim!"

"Yes, you can! Point your toes, kick your legs — Careful! Don't drop the urn again! Don't slouch and don't forget to breathe!"

I kicked and breathed and hoisted the urn above my head.

"Good! Now follow me." She swung her arms in graceful strokes then her feet kicked a spray of water into my face.

Spluttering and floundering I miraculously made it to shore without drowning.

Once we arrived, I flopped onto the good, solid ground and heaved a sigh of relief.

"That wasn't so bad, was it?"

I groaned. "Easy for you to say."

"Now you can tell the silly sentries back home that you swam away from pirates and lived to tell the tale!"

I sat up and looked upon the clear water. Some of the sunken buildings peeked out above the surface.

"It's too bad people can't just visit this place," I said. "That cathedral is lovely!"

Far away, several blue heads popped up and shouted something I'm glad I couldn't catch.

"Who wants to visit pirates?" the princess replied, unscrewing her helmet. "Except us, of course."

I fitted the empty urn back into my bag. "Does the urn have a lid?"

"What?" she asked.

"After we get to the You Know What, how will we keep the water inside the urn?"

She bit her lip. "I hadn't thought of that." She avoided my gaze. "Well, you know what they say, 'There's always something you forget to pack.'"

"Indeed," I said. The book on folding clothes for long journeys had mentioned the maxim.

"I guess we'll have to burn that bridge when we come to it." She stuffed her helmet into her knapsack. "The sun is against us now. The sooner we get on the good side of the griffins the better. It's time to face the Formidable Forest."

Chapter 6

What the Griffins
Thought of Our Gift

My soggy shoes squelched with each step over the soft mosses and fallen pine needles bedding the forest floor.

"It's a good thing," Princess Chel said, "that we *want* the griffins to know we are coming. The whole forest can hear you!"

We stopped for lunch, and I discovered a patch of berries. Based on my book research, I surmised the berries were not poisonous, so we harvested plenty for future provisions.

As we walked on, I gazed overhead at the steep trees and reaching branches. Patches of sunlight blinded me through breaks in the leaves.

"Princess, I mean, Chel," I began.

"Hmm?"

"Is a griffin's good side the front eagle half or the lion back half?"

"What?" She shot me a quizzical look. "First of all, 'getting on their good side' is just an expression, and second of all those traditional eagle and lion griffins aren't the only kinds in this forest."

We continued trudging deeper into the woods.

"What happens," I ventured to ask, "if we don't get on their good side?"

She was silent for a moment, her hand idly picking a scab on her cheek. "Then I hope you don't mind walking for a few extra months."

Extra months? I gulped at the thought. My cheeses certainly would not sustain us for *that* long.

"Through uncharted territory," she continued. "There's no telling what might be in the space where we have no map to guide us. That's why we need the griffins."

Something dark flew overhead.

"How exactly will we find them?" I asked.

Princess Chel stopped. "I think they've already found us."

I lifted my gaze up the trunk of a rotting tree, past the winding poison ivy, and to the last thick, solitary branch bereft of leaves.

Two large vultures stared at us, their talons gripping the softened tree bark. The tiger stripes on their back halves rippled with easy breathing. Two long tails flicked like slow snakes. Feathers stuck up around their necks like lavish collars. Their bald heads wrinkled as they narrowed their eyes.

"I must speak to your leader," the princess said bowing. She elbowed my knee, and I bowed as well.

I heard flapping wings and falling bits of tree bark, and before I could look up, my shoulders were seized from behind!

Enormous talons wrapped around the tops of my arms, and with a cold rush of winged wind, the beast lifted me into the air.

I cried out in alarm.

"Hush, Reggie, we'll be all right!" the princess hollered from my left. "Haven't you always wanted to fly?"

I looked down at the trees whizzing past and the ground below growing ever distant.

"No, I haven't!"

* * *

Our torturous flight came to an end, and we were deposited in a grassy clearing. Thin, tall trees formed a canopy over the area, leaning in as if to watch us. A massive slab of rock jutted out as the centerpiece.

My arms ached and tingled now that my blood flowed again.

It ran cold.

Shadowy shapes of griffins appeared high up on the branches. Silent wings folded, and more talons gripped the tree bark. A regal peacock griffin with the hind of a blue and purple leopard stood on the high rock.

Princess Chel knelt and opened her knapsack. My shoes whined loudly as I knelt beside her. She laid out the seven shiny golden claw tips on a patch of vibrant green moss. The embossed gold shone with jewels. She reverently lifted her gaze.

"Good Griffins," she said in the most queenly tone I'd ever heard, "we offer to you this gift and seek your allegiance to us on our noble quest."

Several griffins alighted from the trees and glided to the forest floor. The peacock adjusted his iridescent wings, sighed and remarked to the others, "Not again."

I blinked in surprise. I didn't know griffins could talk!

A small horned owl with the hind of a tabby house cat piped up, "Whose bright idea was it to say we wanted dumb, golden claw tips?"

"And why seven?" said another.

"Because," the peacock said, "our lucky number is seven."

"We all know that, genius!" the owl said. "But it's so impractical! We've each got sixteen claws. What good are seven tips?"

"And even if they brought two sets," another said, "that's only fourteen!"

"And seven more would be too many!"

The peacock ruffled his wings. "Do we have to have this discussion every time someone shows up asking for our help?"

The owl strutted toward us. "Not only are they impractical, but they are hideous!" He picked one up with his talons. "When it comes to jewelry, I prefer silver." He turned and stared at my chest. "Like the fancy buttons he's got."

My stomach shriveled.

"Enough!" the peacock said. "What do you suppose their quest is?"

"I've heard about this girl," said a flamingo griffin flicking a bushy, pink tail with a black tip. "She's a princess."

More voices joined in.

"Took on dragon Smelter Number Three!"

"Single-handedly!"

The peacock said, "But why does she need our help, do you think?"

I wondered why the peacock didn't just ask her himself. I also wondered why the princess didn't offer any explanation; she just sat patiently watching them.

"You know what we should have done," the owl said, flicking his tabby tail, "We should have spread a legend asking for food!"

"Yeah," said the flamingo, "like seven loaves of bread!"

"Or seven homemade pies!"

The two vulture griffins that carried us here began circling behind our backs.

One of them said, "Now I'm getting hungry."

The back of my neck prickled. Next, they might claim seven of our limbs to eat!

Not on my watch.

"I have seven types of cheese," I piped up, a tad more shrilly than I care to admit.

All the griffins froze.

The princess stared at me with a look of horror.

The griffins stared at me with looks of horror.

Princess Chel whispered under her breath, "Why did you say that?"

"Because," I whispered back, "they want food not jewelry."

"No, they don't!"

"Yes, they do!" I scoffed. "Haven't you been listening?" I looked at the owl griffin. "Isn't that what you said?"

He stared at me, and his beak dropped open. "He can understand us."

"Of course, I can understand you," I said.

"You can understand them?" Princess Chel gasped.

All the griffins stepped closer, staring wide-eyed at me.

I swallowed. "Do...people normally... understand griffins?" I asked.

In unison, the princess and all the griffins said, "No."

Chapter 7

Lucky Me

The peacock griffin flew down from his high rock and landed before us with fierce majesty.

"Who are you?" He looked at me sideways, flicking his iridescent blue leopard tail. His deep-colored eye seared into my very soul.

"Reginald Fitzhamlet the Seventh," I offered in a small voice.

Chattering erupted among the griffins. "The seventh!"

"When were you born?" the peacock turned to look at me with his other eye.

"July 7th."

They gasped.

"How many siblings do you have?"

"Six older sisters."

They were silent. Nobody moved.

"Reginald Fitzhamlet," the peacock rose onto his hind legs, flaring out his shimmering wings. "You are the luckiest man alive!"

The griffins cheered.

I raised my hand, and they quieted down.

"What does that mean, exactly?"

"It means that because of your lucky sevens, you can understand our language." The peacock stretched out a wing and motioned me to stand, "All of us are forever at your service."

The griffins, big and small, high and low, all fanned their wings, raised their tails, and bowed.

A swell of pride warmed my chest as I stood there. I wasn't used to such attention. Even the Princess still knelt.

"Let's hear it for the lucky fellow!" The peacock let out a resounding squawk, and the others all joined with their own birdcalls. Some flew in and out of the trees and some leapt, dancing across the forest floor with loud whoops of celebration.

Something tickled my legs.

I froze and glanced down. The owl tabby cat was humming a combination of a purr and a coo as he rubbed against my shins.

A swarm of other griffins followed suit, brushing against me from all possible sides.

A giant, fluffy, pink tail bashed me in the face.

I decided attention is overrated.

"Reggie," Princess Chel called, "does this mean we made it on their good side?"

The griffins laughed and transferred their attention to the princess

"I believe it does, Your Majesty."

* * *

Once the excitement settled down, some of us gathered on a bed of moss to get acquainted over a picnic. The peacock was named Demetrius, the owl Puffgan, and the flamingo Felicia.

After making a spread of hardtack crackers, cheese, and berries, I acted as interpreter between the princess and the griffins.

"So, what you're saying is," the peacock Demetrius said, "that you want to be flown to the mountains and back?"

"Indeed," I said, "and how long do you think the journey will take?"

"Hmm," Demetrius cocked his head. "What would you all say? Day-and-a-half?"

"Yes," they all agreed, nodding. "Give or take."

"Oh! Is that all?" I said.

"Sure," Puffgan said. "That map you've got is all wrong. There's no hole in the landscape like that!"

"And," said Felicia, "it doesn't even show the Gnome Valley at all."

"Gnome Valley?" I said.

"What's that?" Princess Chel asked.

"The valley where the gnomes live," Felicia said.

"The valley where the gnomes live," I repeated for the princess.

"What are gnomes?" she asked.

"What are gnomes?" I repeated.

"I can understand her just fine, Lucky Man!" Felicia laughed. "Gnomes are little people who manufacture things and live in the valley. It's the ideal spot for a stopping point since we'll need to stay there for the night."

"Wonderful!" I said.

"Those gnomes though," Puffgan made a sandwich with two crackers, cheese, and berries, "they're tenacious little devils!"

Felicia hummed in agreement. "Try to rob you blind!"

"Could sell water to a mermaid!"

"Are they dangerous?" I said.

"Is who dangerous?" Princess Chel said.

"Dangerous to your wallet," Puffgan laughed. "Keep a sharp eye!"

"What did they say?" Princess Chel elbowed me.

"To watch our eyes and pockets around the crafty gnomes," I said.

"Crafty, eh?" She cracked her knuckles.

"If we leave first thing in the morning," said Felicia, "we could get there before sundown tomorrow."

"Splendid!" I said. "Let's set out first thing in the morning!"

"And I'll come along to keep you company," Puffgan said, nibbling some Parmesan. "I got nothin' better to do!"

Demetrius said, "Good luck to you on your journey."

"Aren't you coming with us?" I asked.

"I do not fly long distances. Felicia can take the both of you."

The flamingo griffin proudly fanned her black-tipped wings and bowed with a flick of her bushy, black-tipped tail.

Demetrius ruffled his feathers giving a small bow. "I look forward to our next meeting, Lucky Man."

He departed, and we spent the rest of the day hiking with Puffgan as he guided us around lovely waterfalls and other woodland attractions.

We spent the night in two custom built nests. The exertion of the long day and comfort of the feather bed gave me a sound rest. It was the first night I'd ever spent away from home.

* * *

In the morning, we prepared for our flight. The last time that I had ridden on the back of an animal with another person was when my sister Tilly and I took our cow to market. I was only three.

On the back of Felicia, the princess took her seat in the front with confidence. I climbed on behind and tentatively placed my hands on her shoulders.

"You'll fall off holding on like that!" she said. "Here, I'll switch my knapsack around to the front, and you can hold onto my waist."

As we got situated, Puffgan raised his eyebrows—or feathers, I suppose—and gave me a look.

"Lucky Man!" he hummed.

"What did he say?"

"Nothing," I replied to the princess.

Felicia crouched and tested her footing as if preparing to pounce. "Ready?"

"I suppose," I said.

"Off we go!" She leapt into the air, crashed through the treetops, and soared into the sky.

I would have liked to admire the view, but Princes Chel's hair flew into my face. Puffgan soared along beside us whistling some tune and seemed very pleased with himself.

Chapter 8

Knives, Socks, and
Shiny Windows

As the sun adorned the darkening silhouettes of the Westley Mountains, a green valley polka-dotted with red came into view below.

"Now remember," Puffgan said, flying beside us, "don't let the gnomes talk you into buying anything!"

We soared down into what looked like a clearing but proved to be a field of chopped trees and thousands upon thousands of tomato plants.

I wrinkled my nose.

Bright colored roofs capped the cutoff tree trunks and hundreds of little chimneys puffed smoke, blowing like clouds atop the leafy green tomato shoots. Leaves shook and shivered as Felicia delicately landed, and Puffgan alighted onto my shoulder.

All around us, windows and doors in the houses popped open, and curious little faces peeked out at us. Or at least I think they peeked, I couldn't see any of their eyes because their red and yellow hats sank down and rested on their round noses. Their beards grew down to points much like their funny, pointy hats.

For a moment, they all just stared at us—well, I think they stared. Like I said: no visible eyes.

"Well, what do ya know?" one gnome said from the ground in front of us. "We've got visitors!"

They all cheered.

"Come, come," the gnome said, "let's make our guests at home!"

"How very kind," Princess Chel said, dismounting from Felicia. "We are in fact in need of a place to spend the night."

"I know the perfect place!" said the gnome. "I'm Swingley, and I can show ya to my inn!"

* * *

We followed Swingley through avenues of houses. The roofs reached to about the height of my chest, and all the gnomes bustled around us cheerily advertising handcrafted inventions.

68

"Might I interest you in the latest and greatest set of carving knives?"

"Ever step in a puddle and have to change your wet socks? Never again with a pair of these mighty fine MopSocks!"

"Are ya ready to meet the next love of your life? I introduce you to the Gleaming Cleaning Shine-All Spray!"

I gazed in wonder as they chopped tomatoes, mopped up spills, and sprayed dirty windows. Eyeing the spray bottle, I opened my mouth to inquire how it worked, but Puffgan nipped my ear and scolded me to move along.

In little workshops scattered everywhere—indoors and out—gnomes worked with determined concentration.

One shoemaking gnome on a balcony reached out and plucked down a cherry tomato for a snack, all without taking his eyes off his work. They all performed with inspiring determination.

After taking another turn in the road, Swingley stopped.

"Here we are!" Swingley announced spreading his arms wide.

"Oh," Princess Chel said.

Before us stood a lovely, wide tree trunk with many windows and cozy miniature bedrooms. A brightly painted sign over the front door read "Vacancy."

"Bingley!" Swingley called, clapping his hands.

The little window-washing gnome set to work spraying windows and wiping them down at lightning speed. They really did shine nicely.

"How much are those spray bottles?" I asked.

Princess Chel jabbed me with her elbow and whispered harshly, "You are *not* buying a spray bottle!"

"But," I protested, "what about the—"

"Excuse me," she interrupted. "Is this the only inn?"

"Yes indeed, Miss," Swingley said proudly. "Always vacant too, seeing as how everyone already has their own home."

"It is lovely, but I'm afraid it's a bit too…small," the princess said.

All the gnomes looked up at us—or at least, I assume they looked.

"So it is," Swingley sighed.

"We told you an inn was a bad idea!" Bingley slung his washrag over his shoulder.

"I never thought we'd have any giants come along," Swingley retorted. "We all thought they died out years ago!"

"Oh not at all," I said. "We—uh—humans are quite alive and well."

"We just need a spot to rest," Princess Chel said, "and tomorrow we will be on our way."

"Let's see now." Swingley popped into the inn and returned with a map. He laid it on the ground and unfolded it. The map was long, vertically oriented, and remarkably large considering how small the gnome was. "Just south of here's a lovely meadow."

"By Jove!" Princess Chel said, kneeling down and digging out her own map.

"Well, what do you know!" Swingley exclaimed. "Your map's got all sorts of stuff to the East and West!"

The gnomes oohed and ahhed, crowding close to see.

"And you've got all the space in the middle!" Princess Chel said. "We really need new maps drawn up."

"Would you mind letting Tingley combine them?" Swingley pointed to a yellow-hatted gnome.

"I can have some for you by morning!" he said. "For a small price, of course."

"Splendid!" Princess Chel said.

"I see you've got a red X marked here," Tingley said, pointing to the princess's map. She stiffened. He continued, "You wouldn't happen to be going to," he shuddered, "the Fountain, would you?"

The gnomes all gasped.

"Um…" Princess Chel paused.

The gnomes leaned in.

The griffins leaned in.

I leaned in.

She took a breath. "Perhaps?"

The gnomes disappeared, hiding behind tree trunks. Swingley darted into the inn and slammed the door shut.

Tingley stood alone and gazed up at us with gravity. "Ancient evil lurks there."

Chapter 9

"Prepare for Anything,"
She Said.

"What evil lurks in the mountain?" Princess Chel asked Tingley, the map-making gnome.

"They say ancient warriors, full of mystery and doom, guard the Fountain to combat any who venture near," he said.

The princess stood up taller. "I'm a warrior myself. And Reggie—," she gestured to me, frowning slightly at my visible nervousness, "is coming with me."

"Well, I'm not," Puffgan said from his perch on my shoulder. "Lucky Man, you never said you were going to the Mountain Fountain!" He jabbed my ear with his foot then flew to Felicia's side.

"What do you mean, you're not coming?" I said, rubbing my ear.

"We're not going inside some evil lair full of warriors!" Felicia said, flicking her tail.

"What did they say?" Princess Chel asked.

I swallowed. "They don't want to go inside an evil lair. We never *did* tell them where exactly we were going."

The princess looked down at Tingley, then at the griffins, and then at me. Her face displayed a look I had never seen her wear before: defeat.

Something stirred within me.

I might have rejoiced in the knowledge that the gnomes and griffins were just as scared as I was.

I might have rallied them together to embrace the mantra, "The Darefull be Careful."

I might have taken the opportunity to turn right around and head home.

I might have.

But I did not.

"Please, everyone," I said, "we've taken this quest on the king's honor. He is counting on us."

Gnomes emerged from their hiding places. The griffins sat together. They all listened expectantly.

I took a breath and stood taller. "Risking life and limb, we swam away from pirates and lived to tell the tale. We learned that the legends about the griffins were false, and they've sworn their allegiance to us. We dared to venture into this uncharted land, ready to face any danger, and what did we find?" I gestured to the gnomes. "We found you! A charming people full of vigor and industry! I'd have never come this far if not for Princess Chelseanna. We will not turn back now. Not on my watch."

A corner of the princess's mouth turned up in a smile.

"Suit yourselves," Tingley said, wrapping up the maps. "I'll have your map ready in the morning."

"I guess we did agree to be at your service," Puffgan said. I perked up. "Within reason!" he added, squinting dubiously at me.

"Of course," I said. "I'm glad you'll be of service again. We'll be careful."

Princess Chel smiled and whispered, "But not *too* careful." She winked at me.

"Swingley," she asked aloud, "my companions could use some dinner before resting for the night. Do you serve food in your inn?"

Swingley cocked his head to the side. "In my inn? Nobody eats inside!" The gnomes laughed. "Just grab a tomato; they grow everywhere."

"Good enough for me!" Puffgan hopped up to peck a cherry tomato off a branch.

Felicia and Princess Chel plucked tomatoes as well.

I cleared my throat, "Mr. Swingley, I'm afraid I don't care for tomatoes."

All the gnomes laughed.

"Neither do we, good sir!" Swingley said. "But there's nothing else to eat!"

I blinked. "Do you mean to say, you eat *only* tomatoes?"

The gnomes cocked their heads.

"Of course," Bingley said. "Do you mean to say you eat something else?"

Princess Chel and I looked at each other.

"Yes," she said, "we eat lots of things." The gnomes oohed in wonderment. "Like these!" She dug out a handful of berries, a little dry now, and she knelt down.

The gnomes walked around her hand oohing and ahhing again.

Swingley tried one.

He paused.

His hat rose up above his nose, and two beady little eyes widened in pure exaltation.

"How about cheese?" I whispered to the princess.

"Better not," she whispered. "The taste might send them into shock."

* * *

As the gnomes led us to the meadow, Princess Chel discussed geography, and I ordered a custom spray nozzle from Bingley.

Once there, we attempted to pitch the tent, but the main support pole was lost back at the bottom of the ocean with the mermaids. The meadow grass and starry sky proved to be fine substitutes for a tent.

Felicia preened her feathers. "I'll carry you to the lair's entrance," she said. "But from there, you're on your own."

"We'll fly around outside for an hour or two," Puffgan said. "If you do survive just holler, or yodel, or something. We've got good ears, and we'll come get you."

With that, Felicia tucked her head under her wing, and Puffgan curled up and settled down for the night. The princess lay on her back, and I relayed their plan to her. She sighed, her hands tucked under her head with her elbows out wide.

"Reggie, I never asked if you *wanted* to come with me on this quest. I just dragged you along! At first, I thought you'd hold my diving air hose and be an extra sword wielder, but you've been much more than that." She glanced at me then looked back at the sky.

"I thought I needed a fighter, but what I really needed was...a friend."

The stars above twinkled a little brighter. I smiled.

She just called me her friend!

She turned to look at me with a serious expression. I mellowed my smile to follow suit.

"No matter what we face at that mountain tomorrow," she said, "thank you for facing it with me."

"Of course—" I almost said, *Your Majesty.* "Of course, Chel."

I turned back to gaze at the sky.

"I never imagined I would go on a quest," I said. "My family has a bad history with quests ever since my namesake, Reginald the First, never returned from one. I had no desire to ever leave the kingdom, but the world is more wide and wonderful than I ever imagined! I know this has been a short quest compared to all of your other ones, but questing is much harder than I expected."

Princess Chel chuckled.

"Why do you go out on so many quests?" I said.

She smirked. "It's funny you ask that. Someone asked me the same question on my last quest!" Her expression became serious again. "At first it was to prove myself. I wanted to prove I was fearless, strong, and capable. But the truth is, I'm not totally fearless. You find strength by challenging your capabilities when you are afraid.

"Back home, I don't really fit in anymore. Nobody knows how to talk to me. I felt more lonely at the party full of people than I did walking home by myself. Returning after a quest is like wearing new socks inside old shoes."

She was silent. An easy breeze whispered through the meadow grass. Gossamer clouds glazed over the moon.

As I drifted off to sleep, I wondered if I too would return home with a feeling of "new socks."

* * *

The next morning we were sent off with a new map and a custom spray nozzle fitted just right to the Bolli-hydrium Urn of Fathomless Depths. The map and nozzle were a splendid bargain, and the princess had *just* enough mermaid gold to cover the cost!

"If you survive," Swingley said, "be sure to come back for a visit!"

"We will!" Princess Chel said from the back of Felicia.

"Wouldn't mind coming back here myself," said Puffgan. "Best tomatoes I've ever had!"

"With luck, we'll all come back," Felicia said as she launched into the air.

The gnomes waved from their tree trunk windows as we soared up and away.

The air amid the mountains was chilled and thin. One peak, capped with snow, rose higher than the others.

Princess Chel eyed her new map then pointed. "Lone Spire!"

A dark hewn archway yawned open, jutting out of the snowy mountainside.

"We'll drop you off on that ledge, Lucky Man," Felicia said, gliding downwards.

"All right, Reggie," the princess said, "prepare for anything."

I took a deep breath.

"Prepare for anything, huh?" Puffgan shrieked. "Did you prepare for THAT?"

An enormous shadow, like an eclipse of the sun, swept over the mountain, casting the entrance in darkness. An avalanche of black scales dove in front of us and the massive form landed on the mountain.

The snow quaked and spilled down in rivulets of powder. Hot steam blasted a fog through the air and a long, armored tail curled across the cave entrance.

As the steamy fog melted away, an all-too-familiar eye stared into my very soul. A ghastly patch, made from a torn house roof, covered the spot where the other eye had been.

A cold knot sank in my stomach. "Is that...?" I quavered.

"Maximus Khanivorous Smelter the Third," the princess said.

"But I thought you killed him!"

"Well," she said, "obviously, that didn't happen."

Chapter 10

You Know Who and
the You Know What

The dragon's one eye squinted in fiery vengeance.

"So, Princess," the dragon boomed, "we meet again!"

Felicia squawked and teetered in the air. Puffgan flew behind me and hid.

I clung to the princess's waist and tried to remember what I read on dragon-battling techniques.

"How on earth did you find me?" Princess Chel shouted at the dragon.

"Engaging in Conversation" was Step Number Three! Why had she jumped past Step Number One: "Try to Escape", and Step Number Two: "Try *Another* Way to Escape"?

"Your Father the King," the dragon said, "has been boasting non-stop about your quest. It is all anyone talks about."

"Drat, Daddy!" Princess Chel pounded a fist on her leg.

I wondered if Puffgan and I should "Form Some Kind of Distraction" — Step Number Four.

"How's the old eye socket?" the princess called.

The dragon smiled wide.

I braced myself for an angry blast of fire, but instead he nodded.

"I'm recovering remarkably well from the surgery! I'm flying much better without that nasty double vision!"

"Glad to hear it!" Princess Chel said with good cheer.

"That's why I flew here," he said. "I wanted to thank you personally."

"Wait," Puffgan peeked over my shoulder, "you mean he's serious?"

"Did you," I said, "*help* him?"

"Oh, yes," Princess Chel said. "Poor old Max was in a terrible way when we first met. He hardly could fly anywhere, it was so bad!"

"And just look at me now!" Maximus Khanivorous Smelter the Third flapped his wings, leapt off the snow, and circled around the mountain peak gleefully puffing rings of smoke to fly through.

"Why didn't you fight him?" I said to Princess Chel.

"Because when I arrived, I was so exhausted from my journey, and there he was reposing on his monumental pile of hoarded cushions—"

"Cushions?"

"Yes! The finest specimens of pillow upholstery I've ever seen. Luxuriously comfortable! He invited me to take a rest, and then we got to talking. He's a certified dragon therapist!"

"Before the surgery," Old Max said, beginning to look more like an elderly gentleman than a one-eyed pirate, "with double vision, I couldn't fly very well, so dragons came to my practice for therapy sessions. But now—thanks to you, Princess—I can conduct my anger management classes anywhere! I believe we'll see some remarkable breakthroughs!"

"Wonderful!"

"How is that 'Confide in a Friend' exercise I suggested coming along?" He landed back on the mountain more gently than before.

"Oh…" the princess nervously fiddled with a scab on her blushing cheek. "I'd say it's, um, going all right."

"Wonderful," he said, smiling warmly. "Well, don't let me get in the way of your quest!" Felicia and Puffgan flew us down to the entrance. "I see you have some griffin friends." Max bowed his head. "Lucky to know you."

The griffins perked up.

"Do you speak griffin?" Princess Chel asked as we dismounted.

"Of course," he replied, "my foreign language credit in school."

He turned to Felicia and Puffgan to inquire about their journey and if they would consider spreading word of his services to the griffin community.

"Well, Max, Reggie and I had better be off." They all smiled and waved. "We shall see you upon our return!"

I looked into the dark tunnel

"*If* we return…" I said.

"Good luck," Felicia said.

"Oh, Max!" Princess Chel dug in her knapsack and produced a stick with a rag tied to the end. "Would you mind?"

The dragon blew on the torch and it lit up.

"Thank you!" she called. She patted me on the back and handed me my sword from her knapsack. Then she withdrew her own. "Well, we've already faced a dragon! How bad can the warriors be?"

I was about to say how the dragon wasn't actually bad at all, so the warriors could prove to be very bad indeed, but she sped right along into the cave, holding her torch high.

Dark scorches decorated the walls, in runes, pictures, and words.

"BEWARE!"

"GO BACK!"

"RETURN TO YOUR LOVED ONES!"

Our steps echoed as we walked down a winding, stony ramp. A black, charcoal picture of a forlorn figure appeared to be crying an ocean of tears.

"Who goes there?" a thin, weary voice called from below.

We paused. I gripped my sword hilt tighter.

"We do!" Princess Chel said, extending her torch and picking up her walking pace.

"If you're looking for the Fountain of Eternal Youth," the voice moaned, "don't bother. It's not worth it."

"Don't listen," she whispered back to me, "he's trying to trick us!"

"I'd turn back if I were you."

Another voice, shrill and light, said, "Didn't ya read the signs?"

A splash echoed through the tunnel. A new voice chimed in, "Have we got company?"

"I'm afraid so," said Princess Chel as we emerged into a high-ceilinged cavern.

One massive stalactite hung down, like a chandelier, dripping melodically into a wide pool. Starry bursts among the stalactites cast a quiet, aquamarine glow reflecting off the water illuminating the cavern. Warm steam clouded above the pool rising slowly to the ceiling.

Three figures stared at us: a mermaid, a gnome, and a man.

The blue skinned mermaid lounged at the edge of the pool. Her straight, blood-red hair trailed into the water and fanned out, rippling with the slow movement of her pink tail. The gnome sat on a stumpy rock, holding a shovel like a spear at his side. His pointy gray hat sagged loosely over his eyes and ears, and his beard was woven and tied up in a loopy knot.

A circle was drawn in the dust with little round stones scattered about for a game of marbles.

The man laid down a small handful of stones and stood with a sword sheathed at his side. He groaned, "You young scoundrels ought to grow old while you still can."

He looked to be only about thirty years old himself.

"Are you going to fight us for the water?" Princess Chel asked, sword and torch in hand.

"Fight?" the man laughed. "Little Miss, you can take all the water you want!" We stepped forward. "But," he continued, "only if you want to be miserable for the rest of eternity."

The princess and I glanced at each other and eyed the warriors.

"That's right," the mermaid said, "we tried to warn old Frank when he arrived, but he didn't listen. Did you Frank?"

"Nope, I didn't," the gnome said.

"You regretted it, didn't you Frank?"

"Yep, I did."

"Your friends all left you, didn't they, Frank?"

He turned to face her. "I didn't have any friends. All I did was garden. When everyone

I was mildly acquainted with died off, I came back here."

"After that," the man said, "we spread a rumor saying only old worriers, full of misery and gloom, shirk here."

I cocked my head.

"We heard old warriors full of mystery and doom lurked here," I said.

The man groaned. "I even failed at spreading a rumor!"

"So, if you aren't warriors," Princess Chel said, "how did *you* get here?" she gestured to the mermaid.

"Well now, that's a story." She rested her elbow on the edge of the pool and put her chin in her hand. "I'd gone up from town into the Formidable Forest to pick berries for the Cathedral Music Festival—"

"What?" the princess exclaimed. "How could a mermaid go into the forest?"

98

The mermaid shot her a look. "If you let me finish, maybe I could get to that part."

"Sorry."

"So anyway, I was on high ground when the earthquake hit and the sinkhole swallowed up my whole town into the ocean!"

The princess and I gasped.

"So," the mermaid continued, "I ran away and just wandered until I wound up here. The pool looked so clean, and I was so dirty. I took a long bath, and that's when I discovered that I turn into a mermaid after five minutes of being in the water!"

Princess Chel and I stood there, speechless for a moment. So that was how the mermaids were running after us!

"So," the princess said, "You never swam in the ocean before?"

She gasped and eyed her reproachfully. "Of course not! The ocean is deadly! That's why I ran away."

"Was that four hundred years ago, Maggie?" the man said.

"Probably four hundred and fifty by now," she replied casually.

"So, you see," the man said, turning to us, "save yourselves the trouble and forget about the Fountain. Forget about us. Spread a better rumor than I did."

"What is your story?" I asked.

"Me?" he said. "I'm nobody. A disgraceful excuse for a human being! I set out on a quest to make a name for myself. All I wanted was to be remembered for greatness. But alas, I failed my quest and was too ashamed to return home." He clutched his hand over his heart.

"What was your quest?" the princess inquired.

"To find the edge of the world and peer over the side," he said, "but instead I went in a complete circle! Disgraceful!"

My ears perked up. "What is your name?" I said.

He shook his head and placed a hand over his heart. "Reginald Fitzhamlet."

I dropped my sword. The clang resounded through the cave.

"G-G-G-Great Grandfather?!" I gasped.

He looked at me. "What?"

I stepped forward. "I am Reginald Fitzhamlet the *Seventh*!"

His jaw dropped.

"See!" Princess Chel said. "They did remember you after all!"

I staggered toward him, and he embraced me with open arms.

102

"I can't believe it!" he said. "All these years I never knew I had a family legacy!"

"Come home with us!" I said. "We're not going to drink the water. We want to take it home and spray it on the castle."

"Now there's a novel idea!" Frank the gnome said.

I took the urn from my bag and unscrewed the spray nozzle.

"Oh, but what about Maggie when all the water's gone?" Princess Chel looked at the mermaid.

"I'll get my legs back once I'm dry!" She lifted herself out of the pool.

I lowered the urn, and all the water in the pool and the clouds in the air drained inside.

"And now no one will make our same mistake drinking it!" Reginald the First said.

"But, my dear friends," he turned to Frank and Maggie, "what shall you do now?"

"Maggie could return to the mermaids now that they can walk!" I suggested. "I think they'd all forgotten about their ancestors having legs. Until yesterday."

"You mean they survived?" She clasped her hands. "How wonderful!"

"And Frank," I looked down at the gnome, "you said you used to garden?"

"That's right," he said.

"What did you grow?"

"Oh, just about everything: tulips, vegetables, berries, peanuts—"

"You can bring gardening back to the gnomes!"

"What?"

"All they eat now are tomatoes."

"That's all?" His beady eyes widened in shock, raising the brim of his hat.

"Well, what do you say?"

The three of them cheered, and Princess Chel stood with a beaming smile on her face.

* * *

On the return journey, Frank the gnome rode Puffgan. Maggie and Princess Chel rode Max the dragon, and I rode Felicia with Grandfather. On the way, I told him all about my parents and sisters.

We dropped off Frank and Maggie. Max went on his way, and then the griffins took us as far as the field by the West Gate. A sunset painted the sky.

"Thank you, dear griffins!" Princess Chel said.

"Our pleasure!" Felicia bowed.

"I got a feeling we'll be seeing you soon." Puffgan said.

"What did they say?"

I smiled. "They said we'll see each other soon."

The princess hugged Felicia's neck and leaned down to plant a kiss on the top of Puffgan's head.

He purred and waved his tail in the air. "I definitely won't mind seeing her again!"

She stepped back, and the griffins looked at me.

"Thank you, friends." I said. "I can't tell you—"

"Eh," Puffgan interrupted. "You don't have to! See you later, Lucky Man!"

With that, they laughed and flew off into the sunset.

We turned to face the gate.

"After all these years..." Grandfather said trailing off.

Princess Chel gave his arm an encouraging pat then charged forward.

I squinted to see who was guarding the gate at this hour and to my astonishment, found the bloke—asleep!

I took in a breath to wake him up, but Princess Chel hushed me with a smile. She tiptoed past him and raised her hood to shadow her face.

"Let's not cause a big fuss until tomorrow, shall we?" I nodded. "Good night, Reggie."

"Goodnight—" Grandfather and I said at the same time.

She grinned. "See you soon!"

We parted ways, and I led Grandfather on the familiar path home.

As we stood before the front door, he nervously twiddled his thumbs.

"What if..." he said. "They don't want to see me? Dredging up bad family history and all that?"

"The only bad part about the family history," I said, "was that you hadn't come back."

I knocked.

A commotion began as voices hollered for someone to get the door.

Tilly burst through and squealed, "Reggie's home!"

Mother dropped her knitting, and a tumble of hugs and cheers and questions swept us inside.

As Grandfather introduced himself and told his story, his confidence grew with our family's warm and welcoming reception.

Tilly ran to collect the oldest two sisters and their husbands, Norma jotted down the story, and the twins materialized a cheese sampler charcuterie board.

At the end of the night, surrounded by family and candlelight, I told them all about my own adventure.

I told them about the sights I'd seen and the hazards I'd met. I told them about the fears I'd faced and the friends I'd made.

With proud tears in her eyes, my mother finished knitting and handed me what she had been working on: a pair of new socks.

After everyone else went to bed, I sat alone in my room and rubbed my thumb along the knitted rows of wool.

An idea struck me, and I slid my feet into the socks and then into my old shoes.

She was right.

It did feel different, but not in the lonely way she described. Perhaps because even though I did not choose this adventure, I was not alone.

* * *

In the following weeks, we tidied up and sprayed the castle. Newly printed maps were distributed throughout the known lands. Tourism boomed — no need to wait two hundred years!

Visitors frequented the West Gate, my old post, and I now served as the Griffin Ambassador, interpreting and delegating negotiations between the griffins and everyone else.

Felicia spearheaded aerial transportation tours, and Puffgan oversaw all barter transactions, now mostly food and *not* golden jewelry.

Princess Chel reinvented the Kingdom Sentry Training Seminar to include swimming lessons, conversational dragon etiquette, and geography among other classes.

She also instituted a mandatory quest of at least one night abroad for sentry students to qualify for graduation, and she coined a new catchphrase: Daring is Caring.

Frank thrived in Gnome Valley, making friends by teaching horticulture classes to his kindred who set to work learning to garden with their usual industrious gusto.

Swingley built a new and improved inn with larger rooms. The gnomes also manufactured diving suits of all shapes and sizes for Maggie's underwater tours. (Guests were advised to dive at their own risk and keep an eye out for pickpockets.)

Once the mermaids discovered their legs again, they too traveled far and wide.

Visitors to our kingdom marveled at our famous cheeses and loved walking tours with Reginald the First through the castle and to historical sites.

With so much traffic and commercialism in the castle, the royal family decided to change residence in the summer to the quieter East Side of the kingdom. Their new summer home even had a patio rooftop for small dinner parties, billiards, and a place to sleep under the stars if there was no rain.

On one such quiet evening, I was invited to join the royal family for dinner. In the light of the setting sun, the king played billiards as Princess Chel and I ate cheese and crackers while swinging idly in hammocks.

"Well, Reggie," she said, "we've been home all summer as the rest of the world has discovered vacationing for themselves."

"I think," I said, "things will settle down come winter."

She grinned and gazed out at the East Gate. She pointed. "Have you ever wondered what lies to the East?"

I paused with a cracker and cheese sandwich suspended mid-bite. "No?"

Princess Chel cast me a mischievous sideways glance. "Would you like to find out?"

I grinned. "Another adventure? Lucky me!"

The End

THE KNOWN LANDS

The Westley Mountains

Lone Spire

GNOME
HOME OF VIGOR

Acknowledgements

Most people skip the acknowledgements because it is not relevant to them.

Well, this one's for you.

Yes, **YOU**!

If you are reading this that means you picked up this little book and read it on purpose.

Thank you, Dear One.

You don't know how much that means to me! Unless you can imagine that your willingness to read my story means more to me than chocolate, mashed potatoes, ravioli, and even cheese!

Then maybe you'll know how much you mean to me!

Thank you to everyone who followed along, chapter by chapter, for the first draft during the lockdown of 2020.

I wrote this story as a comfort and humorous diversion for my friends and family. Many of us were out of work. Some of us worked from home, and some continued to work as essential personnel.

When I'm faced with dark times, my gut response is to share stories. They bring a unique comfort and can speak when other words fall short.

When I began sharing this story, I didn't have the whole thing written. I didn't even know how it would end!

On the one hand, it was a very dumb way to write a story, but on the other hand, it was the perfect way to write this story, because just like Reggie did not choose his adventure, none of us chose ours either.

I want to dearly thank my writing friends from OYAN, Asbury, and SCBWI. Your critiques and lessons have shaped and empowered my writing tremendously.

If I named all of you here, it would be like reading those chapters of genealogies in the Old Testament that I always skim over!

There is one lady I need to publicly acknowledge here: Miss Karen, the Reading Doctor.

She read my books from kindergarten to my senior year of high school with gaping wonder and smiling pride. Our assessment sessions each year officially determined if I passed to the next grade, but unofficially they were "Show-and-Tell with Miss Karen" time, and I loved it.

I hope that whoever is reading this has a Miss Karen in life who appreciates the areas that enliven you with joy!

Special thanks to Mom, Ben, and Kaylee for being my voluntold brainstorming squad, and to Dad who likes anything I write.

I must thank Megan for editing the manuscript. Without you, Reggie would not have been given a swimming lesson and Puffgan would not have gotten his adorable kiss on the head! Your keen eyes are also better at weaseling out grammar gripes than mine.

I must thank Harpley. Not only is she my illustrator, but she is also my friend. Her creativity and adaptability have brought this story to life and brought tears to my eyes! When I saw the first rough sketches of Reggie, enlivening joy swelled inside, and I felt like a proud mother. Thank you for showing me what my world looks like.

To you reading this, thank you, Dear One, for reading my first published book. I've got a feeling this won't be the last. ☺

Catherine L. Haws

Catherine L. Haws has been writing since the age of five, so technically this is not her first book. Aside from writing, Catherine acts in plays, operates cameras, improvises recipes, and is one of *those people* who talks during movies.

Instagram: @catherine_haws

Emily "Harpley" Steadman is a freelance illustrator who can often be found happily scribbling in sketchbooks. When not drawing, she enjoys mentoring high school students, playing the harp, and cheerfully destroying her friends and family at video games.

Instagram: @harpleyart